# THE

# SECRET of the CAVE

### A Thrilling, Inspiring Mystery Story
### for Boys and Girls

*By* **ARTHUR S. MAXWELL**

Author of Uncle Arthur's Bedtime Stories,
The Children's Hour With Uncle Arthur,
Little Angels Unawares, Uncle Jim's
Visitors, etc.

*Illustrated by John W. Atterbury*

**PACIFIC PRESS PUBLISHING ASSOCIATION**
Mountain View, California

Omaha, Nebraska        Cristobal, Canal Zone        Brookfield, Illinois
Portland, Oregon

# Preface

Looking back across the years I can still see that quaint old village on the northwest coast of Scotland where the scene of this story is laid. I remember climbing down the ship's ladder from the Glasgow steamer into the little rowboat that took me ashore. I can see the villagers waiting eagerly and curiously for the mail—and the passengers—while behind them stood their thatched-roof cottages, all in a row along the shore.

I recall visiting in several of these cottages, also in the gamekeeper's home, the one with two stories and a tiled roof, farther inland. I recall the glorious vista from the top of the nearby mountains, that marvelous view of rolling sea, mist-draped islands, and the setting sun.

Here, in this lovely, lonely spot, *The Secret of the Cave* was born. May it inspire children everywhere to find their greatest joy in helping others, and bringing comfort and happiness to those in need.

UNCLE ARTHUR.

"Twin Oaks,"
101 North El Monte Avenue,
Los Altos, California.

Copyright, 1951, by
PACIFIC PRESS PUBLISHING ASSOCIATION

# Contents

Flashlights on, the party advanced into the darkness.

# Chapter 1

# Smugglers or Spies?

*I*T WAS the talk of the village. Every topic was forgotten save the all-absorbing question, Who was in McCullum's Cave last night?

Old Peter Macdonald, a gray-bearded Highland shepherd, had been out late on the hills with his sheep. Returning by a rough short cut along the rock-strewn shore, he had passed below the entrance to the ancient cavern, and had had the shock of his life.

Many times he had seen the jagged opening of this great hole in the cliff face. In his youthful days he had explored most of its long, dark, silent galleries; but now, to his amazement, he had heard the most curious sounds proceeding from its mouth. Loud knocking, as of a heavy hammer on boards, somewhat muffled, had floated down to him. An occasional indistinct shout had added to his wonderment.

(7)

He had not been afraid, of course; not he, an old Scottish shepherd! Yet he had suddenly remembered the oft-repeated tales about the cave's being haunted, and it had been with rather quicker steps that he had completed his journey home.

Now everyone was talking about it. Who had been in the cave? That it was none of the villagers was certain. Why should any of them want to be in the cave at that time of the evening?

All kinds of theories were discussed and dropped and revived, again and again.

Could it be smugglers?—Hardly. They would not choose a spot so far from any center where they could dispose of their goods.

"Spies!" suggested someone, with all the thrill of a great idea. But what would spies want in that lonely spot on the northwest coast of Scotland?

Longview Village was divided that evening into a number of little groups talking over the event.

Two of the village boys, Oscar and Bruce Maclaren, were especially interested. They were the sons of a gamekeeper who

Old Peter Macdonald was sure he heard noises in the cave.

lived on the outskirts of the village. Their
mother had just been taken seriously ill,
and their father had gone with her to a
Glasgow hospital, intending to remain there
with her until she should be well again. So
the two lads, aged fifteen and thirteen, were
left by themselves. Of course they were

sorry that mother and father had had to go away, but they got along very well together, and greatly enjoyed their unexpected liberty.

Going from group to group, they listened to all the latest versions of old Peter's story, eagerly picking up the new details that were added to it as time went on.

The next day, when the villagers decided that some of the boldest should visit the cave and thus settle the question once and for all, these two boys were among the first to offer to go. But the older men objected.

"No, no," said one. "Suppose there should be spies or smugglers in there, with guns, and suppose they should shoot you; what would your mother and father say to us when they come back?"

Despite the cold water thrown on their desires, Oscar and Bruce begged so persistently to be allowed to go that the others finally agreed, on condition that they promise to follow some distance behind the rest of the party.

At last, on one of those long summer evenings when, that far north, the sun does not go down till after ten o'clock, the expedition sallied forth.

The cave was about three miles from the village. Situated a little way up from the shore, it was somewhat difficult to reach. However, as rough steps had at one time been hewn out of the rock, the approach was easier than it might have been. Fortunately the tide was out, or the company would have been obliged to approach the opening by boat.

A scramble over the broken steps finally brought six men and the two boys to the entrance, not without their hearts beating a little faster at the thought of what might be in store for them. A number of others had come along, but these remained below on the shore. Some shouted to the two boys not to venture up. But Oscar and Bruce were determined to see the thing through; and their father being away, there was no one to order them down.

Flashlights were snapped on and the little party advanced into the darkness. Excitement ran high, and everyone's breath was held, as the passages were slowly and carefully explored.

Keen eyes peered ahead, eager to catch the first glimpse of an intruder, or any sign of recent occupation; but there was none. Once the leader stopped to examine the wall. Bits of rock, in rather greater profusion than elsewhere, were scattered over the floor. Someone suggested a landslide, and this seemed to satisfy the rest. Just as they were wondering whether to examine this section more closely, Oscar called their attention to some curious marks farther on. All went to see them, but they proved to be of no importance. Again the men passed on, examined the last passage, and then made for the entrance, baffled!

Most of the villagers were now inclined to laugh at Peter Macdonald. Some told him he should not come home so late. But the old shepherd remained perfectly confident about what he had heard. However, the "mysterious sounds" soon became a joke, and before long everybody—that is, nearly everybody—had forgotten all about them.

But there was more excitement in store

Who had patched the hole in the boat? Everybody wondered.

for the inhabitants of that little village on the west coast of Scotland.

That very night, a boat was removed from the beach. True, the weather had changed, and a heavy storm had swept the shore, and the boat *might* have broken away; but Scottish fishermen are not in the habit of leaving their craft insecurely fastened, knowing the occasional fury of the

Atlantic winds. Everyone was sure that the boat had been stolen. But by whom? That was the problem.

The excitement can be imagined when, a few days later, the boat reappeared in its usual place, but with a neat patch on its side, covering a bad hole received during its absence.

Two days after this, another remarkable thing happened. A horse belonging to one of the villagers had strayed away from where it had been tethered, and, to the great distress of the owner, could not be found. A general search was planned for the following day; but, lo and behold, when the man went to his shed in the morning, there was the horse standing in its accustomed place! The man was dumb with amazement. He had heard of horses' doing many wonderful things, but a horse that could open gates and tie itself up in its stall was beyond him.

Hardly had the villagers had time to discuss this amazing event when something else happened to engross their interest.

There were a few poor widows in the

village, all of them assisted from time to time by the rest of the community. One, however, was poorer than the rest, through frequent illness. Having been helped a good deal in times past, she was now somewhat neglected, and, indeed, in very straitened circumstances.

Imagine, then, her surprise and joy when one morning she awakened to discover by her bedside a small box of crackers, two loaves, and a number of fine herring! Despite the most searching inquiries from end to end of the village, not a soul was found who claimed any responsibility for the kindly action, or any right to the profuse thanks the poor old widow was ready to pour forth to her benefactor.

But where had the good things come from, and how did they arrive in such a place? Was there any connection between old Peter Macdonald's "cave noises," the battered boat, the restoration of the horse, and the widow's midnight visitors?

Longview Village thought and talked and pondered and talked again; and meanwhile events hastened on apace.

A boy stepped from the steamer into the waiting rowboat.

Chapter 2

# "Detective" Roy Arrives

ONE of the weekly excitements of Longview Village was the arrival of the steamer from Glasgow bringing mail, merchandise, and, occasionally, visitors. There was no place for the ship to dock, so it anchored some distance offshore, where passengers and freight were transferred to a small boat and rowed ashore.

It was almost like the arrival of a ship at one of the South Sea Islands; for most of the inhabitants would run out of their cottages to see the boat come in.

A steamer had just dropped anchor in the bay. Through the early morning mist the people on shore watched every movement on the vessel, while a fisherman with a telescope reported details.

"Mails are off now," he said. "Dog coming over. Suppose that's for Peter Macdonald. Don't seem to be any passengers. Oh, yes, there's a boy climbing down—and a man just getting ready to follow. Don't

(17)

seem to know them. P'r'aps they're the
folks that are coming to stay at the store.
That's all. Now she's off again. They don't
wait long, do they?"

As he finished, the steamer began to
glide away to the north and the tiny rowboat started on its return journey.

The two passengers proved to be complete strangers to the village. The man was
a Mr. Wallace, of Liverpool, who had been
asked by his brother, general storekeeper
of Longview, to spend his summer vacation
in this quaint old place. Delighted with the
offer, he had now arrived with his fourteen-
year-old son, Roy, who, needless to say, was
about as happy as any boy would be, with
such a holiday before him.

It was not long, to be sure, before the
newcomers were told of the recent mysterious happenings in the village. Mr. Wallace
did not seem particularly interested; but
Roy—he pricked up his ears to catch every
detail, and felt himself swelling into a real
detective all at once. Here was adventure
waiting for him! Could any vacation ever
have started out more fortunately?

Feeling tired from his swim, Roy climbed on a rock to rest.

At first, he could see no connection between the cave, the boat, the horse, and the
herring. Yet, as he turned the matter over
in his mind, he thought that at least there
might be some slender thread joining the
four mysteries. But what was it? What
could it be? He was determined to find out.

The village being a small one, he soon

became well acquainted with everybody in it. Cautiously he drew from one and all everything they could tell about the remarkable events of the past few days.

Some of the kindhearted villagers sent him up to the gamekeeper's house to find Oscar and Bruce, "lads about your own age," as they said. Not finding them at home, he returned to the store.

That afternoon, he walked along the shore to take a look at the celebrated cave. The tide was low, so he was able to get quite near. But there was nothing to see except the black opening. Somehow he didn't feel like climbing the steps—not just then. Not till he had found out more about it. There was, of course, *just* the possibility that someone might be inside.

That same night, or rather the next morning, Longview inhabitants, Roy included, had another puzzling thrill.

About a month before, one of the fishermen, after much hard saving, had purchased one of the most up-to-date and expensive cork life jackets. To wear his new treasure, and listen to the admiring com-

Slipping, Roy fell with a great splash into the water.

ments of his associates, was his pride and
joy. Then came a sad happening. One fine
evening, when he went home from his boat,
he forgot that he had left the jacket lying
on the deck of his vessel. That very night
a gale arose and the sea dashed over all the
boats lying on the shore, washing away

everything that was not securely fastened, including the much-prized jacket. The man was inconsolable for a day or two, and continued for some time to grieve over his loss.

Picture then his amazement and joy when, on opening his front door one morning, he saw the long-lost cork life jacket right in front of him, securely suspended from a nail. How had it got into such a place? It must have been put there some time after 11 p.m.; for he had not gone to bed till then; and before 5:30 a.m. when he opened the door. However, despite the most careful inquiries, not a clue could be found as to who had put it there.

Roy, with the villagers, was completely puzzled. Who had done it? And was there any connection between all the recent ghostly happenings? Was the cork jacket related to the noises in the cave?

In desperation he determined to forget the whole affair for that afternoon, and go for a good, long swim.

Starting off briskly, he soon covered a considerable distance. As he began to feel tired, he crawled onto a small rock that was jutting out of the water, and rested awhile. Diving in again, he proceeded to another rock, and thence, after a brief rest, to another. Thus he went on, gradually getting farther and farther away from the village.

At last, he felt he should go no farther, and decided that, after one final rest, he would return. Sitting on this last rock, he chanced to look shoreward. To his surprise, he found he was almost opposite the entrance to the cave. The opening looked small, for he was several hundred yards away from it; but it was quite distinct.

And what was that? Surely his eyes did not deceive him! Something was moving in front of the cave! He looked again. Yes, it *was* a figure, but who it was, he could not distinguish.

Unfortunately, in his excitement, Roy had forgotten his own perilous location. As he rose to his feet to get a better view, he lost his footing on the slippery rock and fell with a great splash into the water. When he came to the surface and could again look toward the cavern, the figure had disappeared.

Chapter 3

# The Magic Oar and the
# Mystic Supper

ABOUT an hour later Roy arrived at
the store, very tired, very hungry,
and tremendously excited after his afternoon's experience. As a good detective, however, he felt it wiser to say nothing as yet
about the figure he was sure he had seen at
the mouth of the cave.

After supper, fortified by some good
Scotch oatcakes and rich, creamy milk, Roy
thought he would spend the evening trying
to find Oscar and Bruce, in the hope of getting some information from them. He had
not seen them as yet; but from what he had
heard about them, he felt sure they would
all have a good time together.

He had some distance to walk out of the
village, but, striding along swiftly, he soon
came upon the gamekeeper's cottage. It
was an attractive home, with two stories

(24)

and a tiled roof, quite different from the thatched-roof bungalows in the village.

The two brothers were at home. Roy saw them while still a good way off, and was able to get quite near to them before being noticed. Being real boys, they were enjoying themselves throwing stones at a glass bottle which they had stood up on the granite wall that surrounded the garden.

Hearing footsteps, they turned sharply around, and greeted the newcomer with a cheery "Hello!" Roy introduced himself as the storekeeper's nephew from Liverpool, and this was sufficient to make the other two very interested in him. Some general questions and answers followed. Then all three took up the stone throwing till a final shot by Roy made sure that the glass bottle would never hold water or anything else again.

"I'd take you in the house," said Oscar; "but since father and mother left, it's been getting into rather a pickle."

"We're going to have a proper clean-up the day before they return," added Bruce with a broad grin.

Oscar and Bruce were throwing stones at a bottle on the wall.

"Do you sleep here all by yourselves?" asked Roy.

"We sleep like tops," replied Oscar.

"Don't you feel a bit afraid?" asked Roy.

"Why, no! We've lived here all our lives, and know everybody around for miles," said Oscar, as though he were as old as Peter Macdonald.

"Do you think there might be smugglers or spies in the cave?" suggested Roy.

"Bosh! Have you heard old Peter's story already? Why, several of us searched the cave from end to end, and what did we find? —Nothing."

Roy pricked up his ears. "Were you with the searching party?"

"Surely! We wouldn't have missed the fun for anything. Naturally it was a bit 'spooky'; but then, that made it worth while."

"And they didn't find anything?"

"Not a trace. And didn't we all laugh at poor old Peter!"

The conversation turned to the other mysterious happenings; but while Oscar and Bruce seemed to be desperately anxious to find out who was behind them all, they could offer no suggestion as to how this might be done. Presently the subject was dropped, and Oscar asked Roy whether he would like to go fishing the following morning. Nothing could have pleased him better; and, this agreed upon, he returned to his uncle's home.

The three boys had a wonderful time fishing in the bay.

The following morning, the three spent a most enjoyable time fishing in the waters of the bay. Oscar and Bruce, being experts, soon left poor Roy far behind in the number of fish caught.

"Whatever are you going to do with all these fish?" asked Roy wonderingly, as they landed.

"Oh, sell them!" responded Oscar.

"There are always people who want them, and there are never enough," added Bruce.

"You must make quite a little 'pile' at this game," laughed Roy.

"We do. It swells our pocket money. But what are you going to do tomorrow? Would you like to go fishing with us again?" asked Oscar.

"I'd like to, but I am afraid I cannot," replied Roy. "My dad has planned two or three trips for the next few days, and he wants me to go with him; but after that—"

"All right, when you're free," said the others; and so the matter was left. The boat being hauled up on the beach, the boys parted, Roy going back to the store, the proud possessor of a number of fish, which he soon presented in triumph to his father.

But the thought of the fish quickly faded into oblivion before a new and gripping interest.

"Heard the news?" asked his uncle, as soon as Roy's first catch had received due comment.

"No; anything exciting?"

"You remember that old Sandy lost a brand-new oar in that last storm, about the same time the cork jacket was lost."

"I heard something about it," said Roy.

"Well, last night—he's not sure of the

hour—he felt a big thud on his chest. Looking up, what should he see but the lost oar stuck through the window of his cottage with the blade on the sill and the butt on his chest. He thought he must be dreaming; but sure enough, when he knew he was awake, he found that it was a real, solid oar, the very one he had lost, with his name carved on it. The strange thing is, no one knows anything about it. I never saw anyone happier than old Sandy is today. But it's rather uncanny, isn't it?"

Roy thought it was. He thought more than that. Indeed, his thoughts kept him awake a good part of the night; but he was still unable to solve the mystery.

The following day, he and his father and uncle took a long trip over the mountains, climbing one of the highest peaks to get the view. It was glorious being up so high, looking around at the world beneath. In one direction were mountains, mountains, mountains, as far as the eye could reach, towering one behind another till all were lost in mist. In the opposite direction was the broad expanse of the Atlantic, for once

Old Sandy awoke to find his lost oar resting on his chest.

comparatively restful, spreading away to the distant, indistinct horizon.

Except for the long tramp, the hard climbing, and the magnificent views, the day was uneventful; but not so the evening.

Returning to Longview Village by a slightly different route, they chanced to pass the ancient shepherd's cottage that old Peter Macdonald called his home. It was a typical Highland dwelling, one story, granite walls, thatched roof with two rooms and an open fireplace. Sad to say, there was nobody to clean it up now for his wife had died many years ago.

It was very late when the three travelers passed by the cottage, all weary, footsore, and hungry. Indeed, it must have been nearly midnight. But there was a light shining from under old Peter's door, and as the sound of passing footsteps was heard inside, the door flew open, and old Peter stood on the threshold.

"Who's that?" he called.

"Wallace," was the reply.

"Come here a minute!" cried the old man excitedly. "Come in here, do!" His voice sounded husky; and Roy, as he entered, thought he saw marks of tears on the old man's bearded face.

"What is it?" asked the storekeeper.

"Just this—I never saw the likes of it—no one ever did it before—not for all the long, long years since Mary died. Folks

"Who could have done it?" asked Peter Macdonald.

have been very kind, but—let me tell you.
When I came in this even, all tired and
weary after a long, trying day, expecting
to find just the place I'd left in the morning,
what should I see but everything all different! Someone had had a regular clean-up
—which I'd meant to do many a time, and

never could somehow seem to get round to it—and there was the best fire I've ever seen ablazing in the grate, and on the table —why, Mr. Wallace, I never saw such a spread!"

"And don't you know who did it?"

"No, sir. That's what I can't make out. Who *could* have done it? And what's more, who *would* have done it?"

There was no time for discussion; and anyway, the travelers were too tired for it. So, bidding old Peter good night, they left him in his happiness to speculate as he wished, and hastened home.

But Roy, weary as he was, was not too tired to think. Was this another link in the chain of mysteries? Oh, why hadn't he thought to ask old Peter what he had had for supper! He thought he recognized the odor in the room—but what of that? What possible connection could Peter Macdonald's supper have with the cork jacket, the oar, the horse, or the noises in the cave?

Roy puzzled in vain as he plodded on, his brain soon vying with his weary legs as to which would give way first.

Chapter 4

# The Ghostly Peat
# and the Mysterious Boat

A MOST curious thing happened the following day.

Needless to say Roy did not get up very early after his long trip over the mountains. He was stiff in every joint, and the sun was high in the heavens before he went down to breakfast. Nor were his father and uncle much ahead of him, either.

The three were in the midst of their meal when Mrs. Wallace, who had been serving in the store, came into the living room with a Miss Mackay, a good old spinster of some seventy summers, now shaking from head to foot with mingled wrath and grief.

"Mr. Wallace," she burst out, almost before she was in the room, "somebody's stolen my peat! They have, the mean things! Robbing a poor old woman! It's a shame!"

"It can't be," replied the storekeeper.

Her peat basket on her back, Miss Mackay hurried home.

"Whoever would want your peat? And there's no one in the village who would do such a thing. I don't remember a serious theft all the years I've lived here."

"But they *have* stolen it!" broke in Miss Mackay. "I know they have. I dug it out about a month ago and left it all drying fine.

Then I got rheumatics bad and couldn't go
to bring it home. This morning directly I
got up I went to fetch it and—it was gone!
Hardly a square of it left, though I had dug
six basketfuls at least! It's a shame to rob
a poor, weak, sick old woman like that!"

Poor Miss Mackay was greatly worked
up, and it was a job for the listeners to get
a word in edgeways, let alone get on with
their breakfast. Presently they managed to
convince her that they would do their very
best to find the missing peat, *after* breakfast—and with that assurance she left.

Roy was "all ears" while the story was
being told, and determined to take a prom-
inent part in the coming peat hunt. He
reasoned this way: Six basketfuls of peat
could not walk away by themselves. No one
would take them over the mountains, or
away by boat. Therefore they must still
be somewhere in or near the village. More-
over a quantity of peat like that couldn't
be easily hidden.

Breakfast over, he started out and,
meeting Oscar and Bruce, the three visited
the spot where the villagers dug their peat,

paying especial attention to Miss Mackay's plot.

Sure enough, there was hardly a square left where her six basketfuls had been. Whither had it all gone? The boys spent an hour or two in a fruitless search and then gave up.

When Roy suggested that perhaps someone in the cave might have taken it the other two treated the idea as a huge joke. "Why should anyone in the cave want peat?" said Bruce, with reason.

Arriving home a little disappointed, Roy was met with the most staggering information. Miss Mackay, having chanced to go round to the rear of her premises, which she had not thought to do in the morning before visiting the plot of ground where she dug her peat, had found all her hard-earned fuel neatly stacked up behind her back garden wall.

It was overwhelming. Poor Roy, who had hoped in his heart to find a clue to the other mysteries by solving the secret of the peat, felt deeper in the dark than before.

In the afternoon he went on the beach

and had a quiet chat with one of the old fishermen, John McCorquodale by name. "Old Corkey," as he was generally called, claimed to be the oldest man in the village, older even than Peter Macdonald. He was beginning to suffer from the same complaint as Miss Mackay, "rheumatics." Like her, he often said he "couldn't get about as he used to do."

He was busy repairing his old boat, but found the work a little trying to his back and legs. He was very glad of Roy's help in turning the boat over so that he could tar the bottom, but well repaid him with thrilling tales of his life at sea.

Together they tarred about a third of the bottom of the boat. Then, as "Old Corkey" began to feel some more "rheumaticky" pains, he decided to leave the rest till the next day. So bad did he get that the boat and tar were left as they were, and Roy helped the old man hobble home.

A bright idea then struck Roy. He would get up early in the morning and have the boat tarred before "Old Corkey" could get there, and so give him a happy surprise.

Gladly Roy helped "Old Corkey" tar the bottom of his boat.

Accordingly he went to bed early and got up about 5:30, reaching the boat soon after six. As he drew near to it he rubbed his eyes and pinched himself, to make quite sure he was really awake—for there it lay, just as he had left it the night before, but *completely tarred!* Of course, it was possible that "Old Corkey" might perhaps have been there first. But, no; on calling at his house Roy discovered him still in bed. He made inquiries all around, but no one knew anything about it.

It was uncanny, to say the least. Indeed, it began to look as if some of the villagers must be right when they affirmed that an angel must have taken up his silent and invisible abode at Longview Village.

Roy, however, was confident that flesh and blood—though perhaps with an angelic heart—were responsible for the recent succession of kindly though mysterious actions. To him there was one supreme question—Who? And each succeeding mystery only strengthened his desire and determination to find the person or persons behind all these unusual happenings.

After the boat incident Roy resolved that if it meant staying up a whole night and patrolling the village all by himself, he would do it, if it would help to unravel the secret.

But things now began to happen in the daytime. While one of the younger fishermen's wives was away digging peat, the cottage being empty, the only clock she possessed was removed. True, it had not been going for a month or so, to its owner's great inconvenience and regret; but she had no desire to lose it altogether and in such a way. Nevertheless it had vanished, and inquiries revealed nothing. Neighbors thought they had seen a strange man pass the house, while others felt sure that none but children had been about the place when the removal occurred; but there was no actual eyewitness.

The clock was gone. But two days later, to the mingled amazement and joy of the young fisherwoman, she returned from a short absence to find it ticking away in its accustomed place, nicely polished and mended, almost as good as new. Of course,

There, among the heather, was a piece of rusty clock spring!

as usual, no one knew anything about it.

Roy was puzzled. He could get no clue at all. He thought of every soul he knew in the village and tried to "suspect" them, but without success. He was certain now that someone was at the bottom of it all, yet he thought it was possible that the events were not connected. Perhaps it was his youthful ardor to be a "detective" that was making him jump to wrong conclusions. He would have to wait and see.

It must be admitted he *was* rather suspicious of a certain youth, about seventeen, Robert Malcolm by name. This lad had been seen on the peats the night before Miss Mackay's fuel was moved. Some were sure he had passed the fisherwoman's house about the time the clock was restored. Some remembered he had been out late of nights recently. Could he be the one? It was possible. He was a very quiet lad and didn't mix with the other boys very much. Roy would watch him closely.

Thinking deeply, he wended his way the following evening out of the village southward, in the direction of the cave. This way, after less than a mile, the ground rose steeply and the boulder-strewn hillside made walking rather difficult. Roy climbed some distance up and then, feeling too tired for a purposeless climb, turned to descend.

He looked on the ground to make sure of his footing, and, as he did so, something strange lying on the top of a cluster of heather attracted his attention.

He stooped and picked it up. It was a piece of rusty clock spring!

Chapter 5

# Mystery at the Manse

THAT night a storm blew in from the Atlantic and when Roy awoke in the morning the world was soaking wet. As he looked out of the window rain was still falling in torrents. Every now and then a gust of wind lashed it against the windowpanes. Close by he could hear the thunder of great waves upon the beach.

What a day! thought Roy. He had hoped to follow up the clue he had found in the heather the previous afternoon, but this was impossible now. There was nothing to do but stay indoors and wait for the storm to blow itself out.

After breakfast, for want of something better to do, he went into the store and looked around at all the miscellaneous things his uncle had for sale. Groceries in one corner; pots, pans, and dishes in another; brushes, shovels, forks, and other

(45)

"Who can tell?" asked Dr. MacGregor. "I'd like to know."

garden tools in another. Here and there
were coils of rope, kegs of nails, pots of
paint. It was a general store indeed, in-
tended to supply all the needs of the village.

But few were the customers this day.
Everybody had the same idea about staying
at home till the rain stopped. Now and then,
however, some brave soul, dripping wet,
hurried in to purchase some much-needed
item.

Once inside, no one wanted to go out
again. The customers merely stood around
and talked, hoping the weather would clear
up. This gave Roy a chance to ask a few
questions he had on his mind.

"Have you heard of the strange things
that have been going on in the village?" he
asked one old lady, tightly wrapped in a
shawl.

"Och aye, my boy," she said; "but I dinna
believe a word of it. And I ain't goin' to
believe it till I sees something or hears
something myself."

"But what about Peter Macdonald?"
asked Roy. "What about 'Old Corkey' and
his boat?"

"Nonsense!" exclaimed the old lady. "Peter Macdonald's dreaming, and as for 'Old Corkey,' he may have been drinkin' for all I know. I wouldna believe either of them."

"Well, I would," said another old lady who had just come in. "I know them well. They're good men. They wouldna tell a lie. Neither of them. I'll tell you something *is* going on in this village and I'd like to know who's behind it all. Maybe it's angels and maybe it's not. But something *is* going on."

"Angels!" said the first old lady. "I'll never believe it!"

"Better wait and see," said a weather-beaten fisherman sitting on an apple barrel. "Don't yer be too certain. I've never seen anything like it. Take 'Old Corkey's' boat for instance. Who tarred it? Tell me that!"

And so it went on all the morning and far into the afternoon. Just before closing time the door burst open, and who should be blown in by the wind but the minister from the manse—none other than Dr. Samuel MacGregor himself.

At once everybody in the store smiled a

greeting, for they liked and respected their minister. His coat collar was turned up and his black ministerial hat was dripping water, and this made it hard for Roy, who had never seen him before, to know exactly what he was like. But it was clear that he was tall, middle-aged, with gray hair and a long, serious face—yet not too serious. For there was a twinkle in his eye as he talked with the villagers and told Mr. Wallace what he wanted.

"Sorry to bother you on a day like this," he said. "But the storm has blown down a tree beside the manse and a branch has gone through one of the windows."

"How big?" asked Mr. Wallace.

"Not very big. It's one of the small panes, but the rain is coming in at a great rate and making an awful mess in my living room. Could someone come and fix it tonight?"

"Not tonight," said Mr. Wallace. "But I'll find you a piece of wood you can nail over it and I'll have someone up there first thing in the morning to put in a new piece of glass."

4—S.C.

"Thank you, thank you very much," said the minister, accepting the piece of wood. "I can nail this on myself, and I'll be expecting someone in the morning."

He was about to open the door when Roy stepped up to him.

"Excuse me, sir," he said, "but have you any idea about the strange things that have been happening in the village of late?"

"Ha, ha, ha!" laughed Dr. MacGregor. "Now don't you worry your young head about such things. I've heard about them, of course; but how should I know who's responsible?"

"Do you think it's angels?" asked one of the old ladies.

"Now, who can tell?" said the minister smiling. "Who can tell, I'd like to know?" And with this he opened the door and stepped out.

"Just a minute, sir," called the weather-beaten fisherman from his apple barrel. "I'd like to ask you a question, if I may."

Dr. MacGregor came in again and closed the door. "What is it, my man?" he said.

"I want to know when you are going to

Everybody seemed to be hurrying uphill toward the kirk.

get the bell fixed on the kirk. I like going
to meeting to the sound of a bell and we've
nae heard that bell for more than a month
now."

"I want to get it fixed as much as you
do," said the minister. "Indeed, it would
have been mended long ago if I could have
found someone to do the job. But nobody
seems to know what's the matter. It has
stuck. But I'll get it going again someday.
Don't worry. Good-by, all."

With this he was gone, leaving the group in the store to talk about the storm, the church, the bell, and their minister.

It was very late that evening before everyone had gone home and Mr. Wallace was able to lock up his store for the night. By this time the storm was abating and in all the cottages of Longview Village people hoped that this would be a quiet night when good folks could get their rest and sleep.

But it was not to be. Early in the morning, before dawn had broken, a bell began to ring.

Roy heard it first and he sat up in bed wondering what it could mean. Perhaps he was dreaming. But no, the bell still rang. He jumped out of bed and ran to his uncle's room.

Mr. Wallace was already up.

"What is it?" asked Roy.

"It's the bell on the old kirk!" said Mr. Wallace. "Who can be ringing it at this hour?

"Let's go and see!" cried Roy.

"All right," said Mr. Wallace, as the two threw on their clothes.

Evidently many other villagers had heard the bell too, for when Roy and his uncle went out on the rain-washed street it seemed as though everybody was hurrying uphill toward the kirk. Then the bell stopped.

As they reached the gravestones in the yard about the kirk they caught sight of Dr. MacGregor running toward them from the manse.

"What's all this?" he cried. "Is anything the matter? Who's been ringing the bell?"

"That's what we've come to find out," said Mr. Wallace.

Together they went into the old kirk. It was silent as a tomb and most eerie in the dim morning light. There was nothing to be seen save row on row of empty pews, the old oak pulpit, and—the bell rope!

All saw it at once.

"Pull it!" said Dr. MacGregor, "and see what happens."

One of the men stepped forward and pulled the rope. The bell tolled.

"Incredible!" said Dr. MacGregor. "Who could have mended the bell tonight? And

"Look!" cried Dr. MacGregor. "Look at my window!"

in the dark too! Most extraordinary!"

Nobody had a word to say. This was just too much.

All walked in silence back to the manse, where another shock awaited them.

"Look!" cried Dr. MacGregor. "Look at my window!"

"Which window?" asked Mr. Wallace.

"That window!" said Dr. MacGregor, pointing excitedly to a small pane of glass. That's the one that was broken. See, there's the piece of wood I nailed on it only last night, lying on the ground. Mr. Wallace, did you do this?"

"No, indeed I didn't," said Mr. Wallace. "I was in bed asleep."

"So was I," said Roy.

"Then who did it, I'd like to know?" asked Dr. MacGregor.

Again there was silence.

"Maybe it's those angels again," someone said fervently.

"I'm beginning to wonder myself," said Dr. MacGregor. "But look over there! Footsteps! Angels don't leave footsteps! Or do they?"

There were indeed footsteps in the mud. Roy noticed that they led upward toward the mountainside. Yes! And in the general direction of the cave! Eagerly he followed them for some distance only to discover that they disappeared in a pool of water left by the rain.

Chapter 6

# The Surprise Bookrest
# and the Dangling Penknife

PERHAPS the most remarkable of all
the mysterious happenings of this
exciting period in the history of Longview
Village was what happened to little Jimmy
McDougal's invalid chair.

Little Jimmy was the only real cripple
that the village possessed. When quite a
baby Jimmy had fallen and hurt his back,
and from that sad day he had had to lie
down most of the time. Occasionally he was
well enough to sit up, and then he would be
placed at the cottage door to watch the
other children going by to school or play.

Recently the villagers had clubbed together and bought the poor little fellow an
invalid chair, having had it sent all the
way from Glasgow.

Jimmy was delighted, as well he might
be, but when the first enthusiasm passed off

(56)

he noticed one defect. There was no place to put his beloved books. He was a great reader, and as holding them up made him very tired he could not read as much as he would have liked.

Then came a day when his mother, going to the closet where the chair was kept, came running to Jimmy with the wonderful news that a neat little bookrest had been fixed to the chair during the night. Jimmy's pale little face beamed with joy when he saw it; it was just what he wanted.

But *who* had done it? His mother did not know. Nor did anybody else. It was just another mystery.

Of course Roy heard about the affair, and talked it over with Oscar and Bruce; but that was as far as it got. Roy did suggest "organizing a search," and to this the other two gladly agreed; but when it came to planning details as to where to search and what to search, all three were silent. Roy did quietly suggest "the cave" but, as Oscar said, it did seem foolish to go to the cave to find the origin of little Jimmy's bookrest.

Many a time had poor little Jimmy longed for a bookrest.

"Well, I have an idea," said Roy, just as he was about to leave. "Tell me what you think of it."

"What is it?" said Oscar.

"One question first. Is Rob Malcolm any good at carpentry?"

"Well, his father is the only carpenter in the village. Why?"

"Do you think he—?" asked Roy slowly.

"What a good idea!" shouted Bruce, interrupting.

"Splendid!" said Oscar. "Let's go and ask him point-blank if he did it."

"No," said Roy. "It would be far more fun to catch him 'red-handed.' You leave it to me."

"All right, Mr. Detective," laughed Bruce, "when you catch him, mind you blow your whistle and we'll come along with the handcuffs."

Then, all laughing heartily, the three separated.

The clock-spring incident Roy did not mention, nor the footsteps he had seen in the mud outside Dr. MacGregor's manse. He felt that these were pieces of evidence of the first importance, not to be idly passed on to village boys, and through them to others, and so perhaps put the person he was looking for on his guard.

He had not forgotten, too, the figure he had seen at the cave mouth on his swimming trip some days before. Could he have been deceived? It was possible, of course, but he thought not.

There was the missing penknife, right outside the window!

But then, what reason had he, as Oscar and Bruce had said, to connect the widow's herring, Peter Macdonald's supper, the returned cork jacket and oar, Miss Mackay's peat, Old Corkey's boat, Dr. MacGregor's window, Jimmy's bookrest, and the piece of rusty clock spring with the cave? None at all. Surely it was all foolishness.

True, he had a little evidence against Rob Malcolm, but after all, it was only hearsay. He would give it all up. But that was much easier said than done, for his mind had been full of the series of mysteries ever since he had landed in Longview Village.

That very night Roy's diminishing enthusiasm was rearoused to its fullest pitch. The mystic midnight workers actually visited his uncle's store!

Mr. Wallace some weeks back had lost a penknife which he valued highly as a present from an old friend, and whose loss he had felt keenly at the time. Now he awakened in the morning to find it swinging on a string outside his bedroom window!

Roy looked upon the event as "bearding the lion in his den"—he being the lion—and forthwith made a firm resolve that he would leave no stone unturned till all the mysteries were solved.

He did not know how near he was to the desire of his heart.

Nothing particular happened the following night, but the one after that someone entered old Mrs. MacIntyre's cottage while she was out attending her sick daughter-in-law in another part of the village. The mystic intruder practically rebuilt the old kitchen table which, despite its fearful ricketiness, old Mrs. MacIntyre had continued to use for many months past, there being no one to mend it for her.

As soon as Roy heard the news he ran down the village street to the scene of this latest happening. Very carefully he examined the renovated table. It was now beautifully steady and strong.

Roy noticed that the weak parts had been screwed together, not nailed; doubtless, he thought, this was to avoid making any noise that might have been heard by neighbors—though the nearest cottage was, he observed, fully a hundred yards away.

Suddenly he gave an exclamation of surprise. "Why, look," he said, "this middle board isn't screwed on! The holes are made, but feel, it's quite loose!"

"Well, so it is, I declare!" cried old Mrs. MacIntyre. "Now I wonder why the good angels left that and didn't finish the job?" Mrs. MacIntyre was a firm believer now, as

Roy switched on his flashlight. It was Mrs. MacIntyre!

were most of the villagers, that the angels were behind all these kind deeds.

"I know!" cried Roy. "Whoever did it was disturbed in his work before he had finished, or else he hadn't enough screws."

"Maybe they'll come back and finish the job tonight," suggested Mrs. MacIntyre.

"Why, yes!" cried Roy, getting very excited all of a sudden. "Maybe they will! Say, Mrs. MacIntyre, would you mind if I were to come here and watch?"

"Of course, boy, if you want to, but if it's angels you'll not see anything."

"But maybe it's human angels," said Roy with a smile. "Anyhow, I'll be here about ten o'clock and wait up in the shed in your yard. Then you leave the front door open a little way and bring the table right up to it; so, whoever comes will see it at once and be tempted to finish the job. I'll have my flashlight ready to shine on them immediately I hear footsteps."

Obtaining his father's permission to stay out late, Roy returned to Mrs. MacIntyre's home and hid himself in the shed where he had a clear view of her front door. The door was left ajar and the table made easy of access as arranged.

Roy was very excited. His nerves were on keenest edge. But as the minutes dragged by his spirits sank a little. Perhaps no one would come after all. He got chilly and "creepy," and when twelve o'clock passed he became very drowsy. Presently his eyes refused to keep open any longer and his head fell down on his chest as he dropped off into sound slumber.

Ah! what was that? Footsteps! Roy started up, rubbed his eyes, and felt wildly for his flashlight. Pointing it full at the doorway, where he heard the sounds, he switched on the light.

It shone on Mrs. MacIntyre!

"Where are you, boy?" she cried. "Did you see him?"

"No! See who?" gasped Roy.

"I don't know. Somebody, though. I heard movements and noises and got up to look. But there wasn't anyone."

"But the table!" gasped Roy, running toward it. "Are the missing screws in place?"

They were.

5—S.C.

Chapter 7

# A Midnight Chase
# and a Clue That Failed

ROY could have kicked himself. Why hadn't he kept awake! Perhaps the mysterious person or persons had come just as he had fallen asleep. What a chance he had missed! How exasperating!

"Have they been gone long?" he asked Mrs. MacIntyre feverishly.

"Can't tell," replied the old lady, "but it cannot be much over five or ten minutes at the most. I got up as soon as I heard the noise, but of course I had to put something on, and then by the time I could get to the door there was nothing and nobody to be seen."

"I'll follow them!" said Roy with determination, running down the garden path.

But when he reached the road there loomed up before him the great big question, Which way?

It was a very dark night, somewhat

misty, and of course Roy hadn't the least
idea which way to turn.

He stood a moment and pondered. There
were four routes he might follow. He could
run straight ahead down the main road into
the village; he could go up the rough path
to the mountains; he could turn down a side
track on his right to the peats, or he could
cut across the fields to his left in the direction of the cave.

Which way should he take?

Suddenly he felt the lonesomeness of it
all; how eerie it was there in the darkness
and silence of 1 a.m., thirty miles, at least,
from the nearest policeman. For a moment
he thought he would go back to his uncle's
home and bed.

But, no, the chance was too good to miss.
He would go on. He would find his quarry
if it meant staying up all night and walking
all the way to the cave.

The cave?

Yes. Instinctively, he chose the route
to the left, and, plucking up his courage,
started at a sharp trot across the fields.
Aided by his flashlight he jumped ditches,

In the beam of his flashlight, Roy saw someone running.

climbed granite boulder walls—which take
the place of hedges in northern Scotland—
and gradually neared his first objective, the
spot where he picked up the piece of rusty
clock spring.

He had gone about half a mile when,
chancing to shine his flashlight ahead of
him, he saw a hazy figure a considerable

distance in front, trotting along about as fast as himself!

Thrilled by the sight, Roy redoubled his energies and ran as fast as his legs would carry him. The next time he flashed on the light for a moment he felt sure he was nearer his prey. He hurried on apace.

He was now climbing up the hill on which he had found the clock spring. The figure was much farther up and occasionally a small boulder, loosened by his hurrying footsteps, came rolling down dangerously near to Roy. But that was nothing to him. His long-cherished desire was on the point of realization.

Then he tripped and fell. That wasted two precious minutes. When he arose, the figure was beyond the range of his light. He tried his best to make up for the delay, but in vain. He ran harder than before for half a mile or so, and felt sure he must long ago have caught up to his prey, but there was nothing to see, nothing to hear. Finally he came to the hill under which was the entrance to the cave, but there was nothing to reward him.

Carefully Roy examined the cocoa. There might be a clue here!

At last, tired and disgusted, he turned and wandered slowly homeward. He still kept a sharp lookout, but he might have saved himself the extra energy. Arriving at the store about 3:30 a.m., utterly weary, he soon fell fast asleep.

When he was fully awake the next day, which was not till nearly dinnertime, his father and uncle wanted to know the result of his night's vigil. Mrs. MacIntyre's story of how Roy had gone to sleep just when the "angels" had arrived, had already reached their ears and caused much merriment at his expense; but Roy retorted that he *had* seen *something*, though, and would see a lot more before many hours had passed. More than that he would not say, and the laugh only stiffened his resolve to complete the solution of the mystery.

He was too tired to do any more "investigating" that day, or even the day following, and this gave him a chance to hear the story of the next "angelic" deed. The strange part about this was that it was identical with one that had happened just before his arrival at Longview Village. The poor old widow who had once received bread, crackers, and herring by the hand of a midnight visitor was again the recipient of a similar kindness, but this time with the addition of a quarter of a pound of cocoa.

Roy visited the old lady. She, of course, was overjoyed at the gift, and could talk of nothing else. He made careful inquiry respecting the crackers and cocoa. There might be a clue here! Then he went to his uncle and asked if he had sold these articles to anyone in his store recently. Uncle *had* sold just this very kind of crackers and cocoa lately, but, unfortunately, to so many people he couldn't remember anyone in particular. So that clue was useless.

Roy now resolved that he would give up hunting along these sidetracks and make one last supreme effort along the line he had for many days thought would bring results. He would search the cave. And he would search it by himself.

With this purpose in mind he began to make preparations, being careful to secure from some of the older villagers as good a description as possible of the inside of the cave, especially concerning the number, length, and position of its branching corridors.

With the information he got from these people he drew a rough sketch and planned a systematic and exhaustive search of the long tunnels and dark recesses of the ancient cavern.

Chapter 8

# The Self=Milking Cow and the Light Behind the Door

S IF to encourage Roy in his daring undertaking, the very morning he had planned for the search a thrilling story was brought to him. Old Sandy the fisherman—whose oar was returned so strangely —had come home from a night's fishing to tell how he had seen something move in front of the cave as he was putting out to sea the evening before. He wasn't near enough to see what it was, but that someone, or something, strange was there, he was perfectly sure.

Then, on top of this, Roy learned that old Peter Macdonald, returning home past the cave late last night, had again heard peculiar noises issuing from it.

Naturally the stories were discredited by most of the villagers, who recalled the vain search already made, but for Roy they were of the deepest interest. He felt more eager than ever to go on his great

(73)

"My old cow, sir, milked herself," said the lady.

expedition and could hardly wait to start.

Yet it was risky. Suppose the "mysteries" should not be connected and the occupants of the cave should prove to be smugglers or spies? The thought of that nearly made him draw back. Was it really worth the risk? For a moment he was tempted to give up his idea. Then he remembered the old saying, "Nothing venture, nothing win," and he summoned up his courage and resolved to go.

Roy planned to start out directly after lunch, hoping to get the whole business finished before supper; but he was considerably delayed by the arrival at the store of one of the villagers who, greatly excited, began to pour out a most curious story.

"Oh, Mr. Wallace!" began the old lady, "I never saw the likes of it in all my days! I never did. My old cow, sir, milked herself. Well, sir, I don't mean exactly that—but it seemed like it. Ye know how bad I've been feelin' o' late. Sometimes, Mr. Wallace, I've hardly been able to get up at all; but I've always remembered old Nancy and tried to milk her regular.

"Then, Mr. Wallace, yesterday morn, when I was feeling about as bad as ever I have felt of late—I felt I *couldn't* get up, but made myself at last—when I went to the door, what should I find but my two milk cans full to the brim and a note beside 'em saying, 'Don't worry about Nancy this morning.'"

The old villager paused for breath, then hurried on.

"That wasn't all, Mr. Wallace. This morning the same thing happened. It's beyond me, sir, as the neighbors know nothing about it. It can't be divils, sir, it can't, for divils wouldn't do a kind thing like that— it *must* be angels, sir, or—or, sir, unless it's ghosts."

"Have you the note that was put beside the milk?" asked Roy with interest.

"That's the stupid thing I did. I meant to keep it; but then, like the foolish old woman I am, I put it on the fire with some waste paper."

Roy would have liked to investigate this latest event more carefully, but he was now seeking "bigger game," and decided to leave

Plucking up his courage, Roy entered the cave.

the "self-milking" Nancy till a later time.
Should his afternoon errand prove futile he
could but follow up this other trail.

Having heard all he thought the old lady
could tell him, he left her to continue the discussion of the affair with the others, and
started out on his expedition.

Four o'clock found him at the entrance

to the cave, standing on the bottom of the rough-hewn steps, looking up at the black hole he was to enter.

Now, it is much easier to *plan* to enter an unknown and perhaps inhabited cavern than it is to walk in when you get there. At least, Roy found it so. His legs weren't quite as steady as they had been a few minutes before.

But reason finally overcame fear, at least to a large degree. He had come to explore the cave—not to stand looking at it—and in he would go.

He climbed the steps, stood in the entrance, and listened. There was no sound save the quiet dashing of the waves on the rocky shore below.

Roy turned on the light, and its brilliant beam shone far into the interior. But it revealed nothing save rocky walls and a fork in the passage some distance inside.

For a moment he had an almost uncontrollable desire to turn and run, but, controlling himself with a great effort of will, he strode in. A few steps brought him to the forked passage.

Looking on the chart he had made from the reports of villagers, he found the division marked. After a moment's thought he decided to take the road to the right. Slowly he walked on, flashing his powerful light around him so that he might carefully examine the walls for any trace of recent occupation. Meanwhile he hummed a tune softly to himself, to help keep up his courage.

The passage, which rose gradually, brought him into a fair-sized room and there stopped. Having examined this thoroughly he retraced his steps, then turned along another passage which he had passed on his way up. This, too, proved to be a "blind alley," so he returned to the main fork, and took the left-hand corridor.

This turned out to be far more intricate, winding in many directions and branching at several places. In many cases his chart did not tally with what he found, and he wondered many times whether or not he should go on or go back. Nevertheless he was determined to do the job thoroughly while he was about it, and made up his mind to look everywhere.

Roy put his eye to the largest opening, and looked in.

He had nearly finished now, and was looking forward to the glad moment when this nerve strain would end and he would live again in purer air and brighter light.

At last he came to the place described by the fisherfolk as "the landslide." Truly it looked like one; the passage at this point was quite different from its usual shape, and pieces of granite, large and small, were strewn about the floor.

Roy flashed his light hither and thither, looking carefully at everything around him.

This section of the passage certainly *was* unlike anything he had yet seen. One part of the wall was particularly flat, so unlike the rest. It looked like rock. Yet—?

Roy looked closer. What was that? He brought his light right down upon it. It was a piece of string! He went to pick it up, but found it would not move—one end was fixed within the wall.

He pulled hard. There was a click. Then, to his amazement, part of the wall moved and a small door opened, revealing another and evidently secret passage. The door was of heavy oak, painted to look like rock!

It was a moment or two before he could steady himself after this shock. Then, having made sure the door could not close behind him, he followed the beam of his flashlight into the blackness.

This tunnel was much smaller than the others in which he had been. Sometimes his head almost touched the roof. Occasionally the sides came so near that there was hardly room for him to walk in comfort. The length of the passage amazed him: and the farther he went the greater grew his desire to turn and go back.

He had gone, he thought, perhaps half a mile, and was about to give up and return, when distant noises brought him to a standstill, petrified with fright. However, as they became no louder he decided to go cautiously ahead and see whence they proceeded.

To avoid exposing himself he turned off his light and fumbled along as best he could in the darkness. The noises became more distinct, though still muffled by distance.

Roy hastened on as fast as he dared. Suddenly, as he turned round a bend in the passage he found himself confronting an old doorway, through chinks and cracks of which a light was shining!

Trembling from head to foot, but buoyed up with the thought that triumph was near at hand, he noiselessly crept toward the door, put his eye to the largest opening, and looked in.

Chapter 9

# The Great Unraveling

ROY nearly dropped with amazement at the sight that met his excited gaze. Beyond the door the narrow passage expanded into a room of considerable size. An old wooden table stood in the middle of the floor, and beside it were two equally aged benches.

In one corner a small peat fire was smoldering in an open fireplace while in the opposite corner was a pile of blankets and rugs. Upon the table stood an oil lamp, also some eatables; and upon the bench beside it, eagerly devouring the tasty food, sat—yes!—Oscar and Bruce!

Roy couldn't believe his eyes, but there were the two boys, think what he would.

Momentarily forgetting his eerie surroundings, he shouted, "Hello, Oscar!"

The two boys jumped as though they had received an electric shock, and fled for the door at the opposite end of the underground chamber. All they had heard was a muffled roar from the darkness, and terror seized them.

Roy threw his weight against the old doorway and it opened, fortunately, inward. Then he repeated his cry, adding, "It's all right; only Roy Wallace. Come back!"

The two returned, pale-faced and trembling, gazing in astonishment at their friend.

"How in the world did *you* get here?" they gasped.

"And what in the world are *you* doing here?" cried Roy.

And that was about all they could say. Indeed, it took quite a while before the nerves of the three boys calmed down enough for them to talk sensibly again. However, going on with the interrupted meal, with Roy joining in, helped a lot.

The food all put out of sight, the three drew the benches close to the peat fire and began to talk things over.

"So you've caught us at last," said Oscar, laughing. "I thought you would someday;

you seemed so determined about it. But I never dreamed you would discover our hide-out here."

"Well, it *has* been a job," replied Roy. "You did well to cover up your traces so completely. I really had begun to think it was Rob Malcolm."

"It's funny you should have caught us this evening," said Bruce. "If you hadn't, you might never have done so, for we had a letter today telling us that father's coming home next week; and that, of course, will put a stop to everything."

"Just in time, wasn't I!" exclaimed Roy. "I'm so glad for that. But, say, however did you find this place?"

"That was a great find!" replied Oscar. "We discovered it months ago and said nothing, thinking we might have some fun out of it someday.

"We were playing about on the hills one day when Bruce happened to trip over something. He looked to see what it was, and found a short length of iron sticking out of the ground, well covered with heather. He tried to pull it up, but couldn't. Then I went

Jumping up from the table, the two boys fled in terror.

and helped him. Presently, after a great struggle, a small chunk of earth came up —on a hinged board—and revealed an opening. We got candles and crawled in, and finally arrived here. No one would ever spot the entrance on the hills, for it's so well covered."

"But the other entrance—that I found?" asked Roy.

"Oh, that came as a matter of course. We went through the other door in this room and followed the passage. We had a hard job opening the one into the cave proper, and broke it a bit. I fixed it up as best I could, and put the string through to make it easier to open from the other side. It was that that frightened old Peter Macdonald. I was surprised to learn that the sound of our hammering had carried so far down the passages; but old Peter's very quick of hearing."

"Did you often go down to the main cave entrance?" asked Roy, keenly interested.

"Not very often; it's such a long way. We were there last night. Once, soon after you came, we caught sight of you standing on a rock looking straight at us. My! didn't we run! Yes, and what a job it was to look unconcerned when you came to our home soon after and found us pelting that bottle!"

"But now," interrupted Roy, his enthusiasm rising as one after another of his problems was solved, "What I want to know is, Were you two behind all the village 'mysteries' of the past few weeks?"

"Now you want to know something, don't you!" laughed Oscar. "Well, Bruce, I suppose we'd better tell him, eh?"

Bruce nodded.

"Seeing you have caught us almost red-handed," continued Oscar, "I suppose we must confess. Yes, we were. And we were so glad to see that you suspected Rob, because we knew you would never catch us so long as you were after him."

"Tell me more," urged Roy. "Did you have anything to do with the boat that everyone thought was stolen? How did the horse get into its stable, and the widow get her groceries? How were the cork jacket and old Sandy's oar returned? Oh, yes, then there's old Peter Macdonald's supper, Miss

One by one, each mystery was solved.

Mackay's peat, 'Old Corkey's' boat, Jimmy's chair, Dr. MacGregor's window, the old kirk bell, uncle's penknife, Mrs. MacIntyre's table; yes, and the clock and the cow and all the rest of the happenings—tell me all about them, do!"

"My! you want to keep us here till midnight!" exclaimed Oscar. "It was all very simple. You see, no one thought of suspecting us—not even you.

"With father and mother away, everyone expected we would surely go to bed early, and bolt and bar the door for fear of 'bogeys.' But we didn't. Sometimes we slept at home, sometimes here, as you see by the blankets. You remember my careful answer when you asked where we slept?"

"Yes, I remember now; you replied, 'We sleep like tops.' "

"Yes, I was always careful never to tell an untruth, even to keep up the fun. Well, sometimes we slept at night, but usually we didn't—making up for it some other time, in here. Then when we thought everyone was asleep we started to work. Kindly Providence helped us to find a number of things that had been lost—although it meant hours of searching in some cases.

"The boat that everyone thought was stolen must have been washed away in the storm. We chanced to find it on one of our expeditions up the coast. It had been dashed against a rock and had a hole in its side. We managed to pull it up the shore high enough to get at the hole, which we soon mended. Then we bailed it out and brought it home—in the dark, of course.

"As for the horse, we happened to meet it on a trip over the mountains. It wasn't very hard then to get it into the stable— except that it neighed so much we thought we would surely be caught.

"The cork jacket and the oar we found some distance down the coast, while on a fishing trip. It was great fun pushing the oar through old Sandy's window; but I didn't know till afterward that it fell on his chest!

"Now, Miss Mackay's peat. Of course, we were the ones who put it behind her back wall at night—never thinking that she wouldn't see it. And then you came and wanted us to search! How we laughed about that!"

"How about the boat that got tarred?" asked Roy.

"That was my idea," said Bruce. "I saw you and 'Old Corkey' start work on it, and then how ill he became. So I told Oscar. We soon finished the job.

"Then there was the clock. I took that. We brought it here and mended it. The spring was gone, but we took another one out of a broken old clock we had at home."

"Did you lose the old clock spring?" asked Roy.

"Yes, why?"

"Here it is," said Roy, bringing it triumphantly out of his pocket. "Found it on the hill, not far from your secret opening, I suppose. If only I had looked closer!"

"If only!" laughed Bruce. "Dr. Mac-Gregor's window was next."

"Oh, do explain that," said Roy. "How ever did you know the window was broken?"

"Oscar happened to pass the manse just after the tree had fallen. He saw the branch had gone through the window and remembered that we had a piece of glass that exact size in our workshop—they're all standard, you know. So we made up our minds to put it in. Easy as a wink. But as for the bell, *that* was a job. We both climbed up into the belfry in the dark and took a good look at the works with our flashlight. Then we saw what was the matter. Somehow the rope had got caught in something, and when we got it loose the bell worked fine. Of course we couldn't resist pulling it a few times, just for fun."

"I heard it!" said Roy. "Woke me up— and everybody else, too. That was the time I saw your footsteps."

"Did you really?" asked Oscar.

"Yes," said Roy, "but I wasn't able to follow them very far. They vanished in a big puddle."

"Ha, ha!" laughed Bruce. "We went through that puddle on purpose to hide our tracks. But now we must tell you about Jimmy's chair.

"That was Oscar's work. He's quite a carpenter, you know. You remember, I told you that Rob Malcolm's father was a carpenter? So he is. That was to put you 'off the scent.' Rob himself couldn't drive a nail straight."

"Don't know about my being a carpenter," said Oscar, "but perhaps I didn't make such a bad job of it. The best thing, though, was Mrs. MacIntyre's table. That was really great—especially when you chased us. How glad we were when our heather-covered doorway closed over us!"

"Why didn't you finish the job the first night?" asked Roy.

"Hadn't enough screws," replied Oscar.

"Just what I thought!" exclaimed Roy.

"The cow is the next important item, I suppose," continued Oscar. "Nothing to that, of course; we just went and milked her for the poor old soul, only watching we did it when no one was about."

"Well," said Roy, when all his "mysteries" had been unraveled, "you certainly have had a most interesting time of it. But, say, whatever made you do it?"

"I wondered if you would ask that," replied Oscar. "Several reasons. We wanted to make use of our secret chamber in some way or other, romantic if possible. Then, too, we wanted to make the best use of the time we knew we would have to ourselves while father and mother were away. We talked it over and hit on this plan—

Helping others, as Jesus did, always brings happiness.

of helping the sick and poor of the village as much as we could. We thought it would be a fine thing to bring a little sunshine into the lives of some of the old folks before they leave us. You know, 'inasmuch—' "

"That was it," said Bruce. "We thought we would like to put into practice what Jesus said His people should do—feed the hungry, help the poor, cheer the sad. We remembered His beautiful words, 'Inasmuch as ye have done it unto one of the least of these My brethren, ye have done it unto Me.' Yet we wanted to do it without having to go through the agony of being thanked all the time. That's tough to take, you know."

"You're right it is," said Roy, "but I'm sure you *would* be thanked if the village folks ever found out that you two were back of all these kind deeds. Most of them think angels are responsible for them all."

"Hardly angels!" said Oscar, with a laugh. "As to the thanks, they don't matter a bit. We're only too pleased our plan has succeeded in making some of the needy ones so happy. I suppose now that father is coming back we shan't have a chance to keep this up, at least not in the same exciting way; but, anyhow, these last few weeks have been the happiest we've ever enjoyed in all our lives."

So the three boys talked on till the fire went out and the lamp burned dim, going over and over their recent adventures: two of them happy that their efforts to cheer others and brighten lonely lives had been appreciated, and the third rejoicing that at last he had solved the Secret of the Cave.